KING-SMITH, DICK
PRETTY POLLY /

1992.
37565027495745   CENT

DICK KING-SMITH

Pretty Polly

illustrations by Marshall Peck

CROWN PUBLISHERS, INC. • *New York*

Sonoma

Published in the United States of America by Crown Publishers, Inc.,
a Random House company, 225 Park Avenue South, New York,
New York 10003
Originally published in Great Britain in different form by
Penguin Books Ltd. in 1992
CROWN is a trademark of Crown Publishers, Inc.
Manufactured in the United States of America
Library of Congress Cataloging-in-Publication Data
King-Smith, Dick.
Pretty Polly / Dick King-Smith.
p.   cm.
Summary: When she is not allowed to have a pet parrot, Abigail
teaches a barnyard hen to talk.
[1. Pets—Fiction. 2. Chickens—Fiction.] I. Title.
PZ7.K5893Pr   1992
[E]—dc20   91-42449
ISBN 0-517-58606-1 (trade)
0-517-58607-X (lib. bdg.)
10 9 8 7 6 5 4 3 2 1
First U.S. Edition

Contents

CHAPTER 1
A Brood of Chicks

"Pretty Polly!" said Abigail to the parrot in the pet shop.

The parrot said nothing.

"Perhaps he doesn't talk," said Abigail's mother.

"Oh, yes, he does," said the owner of the pet shop. "He's a good talker, he is. You ask him the right question, he'll answer. Ask him his name."

"What's your name?" said Abigail.

"Peter," said the parrot. "What's yours?"

"Abigail."

"Ha, ha, ha, ha!" said the parrot. "What a stupid name!"

"Don't worry," said the shopkeeper, smiling. "He says that to everyone."

"What else can he say?" asked Abigail.

"Oh, lots of things," said the shopkeeper. "Can't you, Peter?"

"Silly old fool," said the parrot.

"Sorry," said the shopkeeper. "He's in a bad mood today. What's the matter, Peter? Get out of bed on the wrong side, did you?"

"Don't be cheeky," said the parrot. "Silly old fool!" And turning slowly around on its perch so that its back was toward them, it made a loud and squelchy mess on the floor of the cage.

"I wish I had a parrot," said Abigail as they drove home.

"You've got loads of pets already," her mother said. "Look what I've just had to buy in that shop—dog biscuits, rabbit mixture, hamster food, ants' eggs for the goldfish. And then there are all our other animals."

Abigail's father was a farmer, and they kept cows and pigs and sheep and chickens.

"Yes, but none of them can talk," Abigail said. "That parrot spoke as clearly as anything, just like a human. I wish we could buy him."

"Did you see the price tag on the cage?" her mother said.

"*How* much?" said her father that afternoon.

They were all sitting around the big wooden kitchen table—Abigail, her parents, her younger sister, Prudence, and her little brother, Bob.

"Eight hundred and fifty pounds."

"Good heavens!" her father said. "You can for-

get about that, Abby. I could buy a cow for that much. Eight hundred fifty pounds for a bird!"

"But it could talk, Dad."

"Yes, and why? Because somebody taught it to, that's why. An ordinary parrot out in the jungle can't talk. Someone spent ages—months and months probably—saying the same things over and over again to that bird when it was young, till it learned them by heart. You can only teach a young one."

"After all," said his wife, "that's how children

learn to speak, isn't it? Listening to what grown-ups say and copying it. That's how you and Prudence learned to talk, Abigail."

"And me," said Bob.

"And you, Bob," said his father. "You don't know so many words yet because you're little, but you will. A thousand times as many as any old parrot."

"I could save up my pocket money," said Abigail.

"That would take forever," her mother said. "By the time you'd saved that much, you'd be grown up, and Prudence, too."

"And me," said Bob.

"I could help you, Abby," said Prudence. "I've got £3.75 saved up."

"I 'spect I've got a hundred pounds," said Bob.

"No, he hasn't, silly boy," said Prudence. "All he's got in his piggy bank is some pennies."

"One, two, three, five, eight, seven, ten," said Bob proudly.

The children's father got up from the table.

"Forget about parrots, Abby," he said. "If you want to teach a bird to talk, you'll have to make do with one of our hens."

"But Dad," said Prudence, "hens can't talk."

"How d'you know?" said her father. "They

can certainly make a whole lot of different noises, can't they? They've just never been taught the Queen's English. Train one of them, Abby. I would. Now, then, I'm going to feed the pigs. Who's coming?"

"Me," said Prudence.

"And me," said Bob.

"But Mum," said Abigail as they washed up the tea things together, "our hens are all old. Dad said you can only teach a young bird."

Her mother laughed.

"Daddy was only joking anyway," she said. "Imagine training a hen to talk! But that reminds me, Abby, something happened today that you don't know about yet. We had some new arrivals. That old speckled hen that's been sitting on a nest in the stable—she hatched out a brood of chicks this morning."

There were seven of them, Abigail found, three red like their father the big cockerel, three yellow, and one speckly like the mother hen. Already they were running about the floor of the stable behind their mother as she clucked and scratched at the straw. Abigail threw down a handful of corn for her and picked up the speckly chick.

"You're pretty, aren't you?" she said.

"Peep, peep!" cried the chick, but it did not struggle, and the look in its eye, Abigail thought, was one of intelligence.

"Well," she said, "if you're a pullet, which I hope you are, and if I'm going to teach you to talk like a parrot, which I hope I am, then there's only one possible name for you. And that's Pretty Polly."

CHAPTER 2

"Eat Wheaties"

The seven chicks grew rapidly, and by the time they were six weeks old it was possible to tell by the shape of their combs and the set of their tails which were cockerels and which were pullets.

As it turned out, the three yellow—later to be white—chicks were all males, and the remaining four were females.

"Just as well," said Abigail to the speckly chick, "or I'd have had to call you Pretty Peter after that parrot, and that wouldn't have sounded as nice, would it?"

"Cheep, cheep," said Pretty Polly in reply.

All of them had now graduated from peeping to cheeping, but Polly had made no other sound, despite constant lessons from Abigail.

Abigail had thought long and hard about what first to teach her pupil. "Pretty Polly," it seemed to her, might be easy for a parrot but very hard for a chick at the start of its education. She listened carefully to the peeps and later the cheeps, and it occurred to her that the best phrase to start on might well be something with one or two of those "ee" sounds.

The answer came one morning at breakfast. The children were discussing their favorite cereals.

"I like ordinary cornflakes best of all," said Prudence.

"And me," said Bob.

"I don't," said Abigail. "I like Rice Krispies best."

"And me," said Bob. "Snapple, crack, and plop!"

The girls laughed.

"You can't like two different things best," said Abigail.

"I can," said Bob. "I like lots of things best."

"Sugar Puffs?"

"Yes."

"And Coco Pops?"

"Yes."

"And shredded wheat?"

"Yes. I like them more better still."

"I don't," said Prudence. "I'd rather eat Wheaties."

"Eat Wheaties!" thought Abigail. That's it! Those are the words to start Polly on!

And so the education of the speckly chick began.

Already she had become noticeably tamer than her brothers and sisters, for whenever Abigail came to visit them she would bring a little offering of rabbit mixture or hamster food and call "Polly, Polly, Polly!"

At first Polly took no notice of this summons, but as time passed she seemed to recognize the sound of her name and would leave her mother and the others and come running.

One morning Abigail took a few Wheaties from a bag in her pocket and crumbling them before the speckly chick said loudly and clearly, "Eat Wheaties."

Polly pecked up the little pieces and cocking an eye up at Abigail said loudly and clearly, "Cheep, cheep."

"You just wait, my girl," said Abigail. "One of these days you're going to say those words that you've just heard for the first time. Wait till you've heard them a thousand times. It's the start of summer, and I don't have to go back to school for ages, but you are starting school now, Polly."

Abigail crumbled some more.

"Eat Wheaties," she said.

Animal trainers need, more than anything, infinite patience, and that Abigail had.

Animals that are to be successfully trained need

a certain intelligence and willingness, and these, it seemed, Polly had.

By now, at two months of age, she had taken to following Abigail everywhere around the farm, as closely as the collie dog Moss followed Abigail's father. And as often (which was many, many times a day) as Abigail said the magic words, Polly would look up at her, head on one side, and give her such a considering stare that Abigail felt sure the pullet understood what was wanted of her. Now she always answered when spoken to—no longer with a cheep but with something halfway between that and a grown-up cluck.

"Chick," it sounded like. "Chick, chick, chick."

Abigail was worried about this development.

She's not peeping or cheeping anymore, Abigail said to herself, so maybe I should stop saying "Eat Wheaties" and try something else. But no, she thought. I won't give up, not with all the work I've put into it.

So busy had she been with Polly that she had arranged for her other pets to be looked after to leave her free for chicken training.

There was no problem with Moss (who she liked to think was hers), since he dogged her father's heels everywhere anyway.

As for her rabbit, Benjamin, Prudence was only too happy to take him on, and Bob—with a little help from his mother—was in charge of Fatso the hamster. The way that Fatso stuffed his cheek pouches full of food until he looked as though he had a bad case of mumps fascinated Bob, and he would try to copy the hamster. Once he tried it with strawberry Instantwhip and filled his face so full that he did the nose trick.

But the trick that Abigail wanted Polly to do seemed no closer to happening. Patiently Abigail continued to repeat the same command, and obediently Polly ate the bits of cereal, but all she said was "Chick, chick, chick."

Gradually, however, this noise also began to be joined by others. Abigail, who of course listened with keen attention to every sound that the speckly chick made, noticed that unlike the rest of the brood, who still continued chick-chick-chicking, Polly seemed now to have mastered all the other vowel sounds too.

"Chick" might be the principal word, but Polly was also saying "chack" (an angry sound made when another tried to steal a tidbit) and "check" (when investigating something to see if it was edible) and "chock" (when very full) and "chuck" (which seemed to be an order to Abigail to throw her down some food).

There was no doubt about it—Polly was developing a larger vocabulary than her brothers and sisters.

Then one sunny September morning there came a moment that Abigail would never forget. It was the last day of the summer holidays, during which she had hoped desperately that Polly might learn that so–often–repeated first lesson. Tomorrow school would start.

Not that Abigail particularly minded this—she liked school, and so did Prudence. And as for Bob, he was longing for the time two years from now when he would be old enough to go and sing songs and eat a lovely packed lunch and play soccer, which is what he thought school was all about.

No, what worried Abigail was that now Polly's lessons would be cut down, for her teacher would be away most of the day, and then there would be homework in the evenings.

Abigail sat on a straw bale in the Dutch barn that morning looking at Polly, who stood expectantly before her, head cocked, eye fixed on the bit of cereal in Abigail's hand. Polly might not always have lived up to her full name—when she was changing her baby down for feathers, for instance, she, like the others, looked a mess. But now, at nearly four months of age, she had grown into a beautiful pullet, with her black-and-silver-striped plumage and her bright red comb and wattles.

As usual, she gave an order.

"Chuck!" she said.

For some reason Abigail did not obey. She sat there in a kind of dream, staring at her bird and thinking sadly that after all her efforts, only chicken noises emerged from that beak.

"Chuck!" said Polly again, and when Abigail still made no move, the pullet fluttered up onto her knee.

Then as clear as could be: "Eat Wheaties," said Pretty Polly.

CHAPTER 3
"Clever Girl"

"Polly!" cried Abigail. "You did it! You said it! Oh, what a clever girl. I could kiss you!" But she didn't know quite how to—Polly's beak looked rather sharp—so she put the pullet down on the ground and ran to tell the other children. Polly ran after her.

Abigail found Prudence feeding Benjamin.

"Pru! Pru!" called Abigail. "She did it! She said it! Polly said it!"

Bob came up carrying Fatso.

"What did Polly say?" he asked.

"She said 'Eat Wheaties.' "

"Why did she say that?" asked Bob.

"Because I've been saying it to her over and over again, about a thousand times."

"Why?"

"Because I wanted to teach it to her."

"Why?"

"To see if she could talk—like a parrot."

"Why?" said Bob.

"Oh, you silly little boy, Bob," said Prudence. "Stop your 'why, why, why.' "

"Why," said Polly.

The three children stared at the bird.

"Did you hear that?" said Prudence in a hoarse whisper. "Polly said it too. Bob said it four times—"

"And then you said it three times," said Abigail, "and she got it! Oh, Pru, d'you see what this means? Polly's got the trick now of listening to what's said and repeating it."

She squatted on her heels in front of the pullet.

"Eat Wheaties," she said.

"Eat Wheaties," said Polly.

"Why?" said Abigail.

"Why," said Polly.

"Because they're good with milk and lots of brown sugar," said Bob.

He waited expectantly for the bird to repeat this sentence. Polly stayed silent.

"She didn't say it," he grumbled. "Stupid bird. I bet I could teach Fatso to talk more better than what she done." And he stomped off to the farm-house.

His mother was in the kitchen cooking when Bob came in holding the hamster in front of his face and saying to it in an earnest voice "My name is Fatso" again and again.

"What *are* you doing, Bob?" his mother said.

"Teaching him to talk. Like Abby's chicken."

"What *do* you mean?"

"Abby's chicken can talk."

"Oh, you silly little boy, Bob," said his mother. "Whoever heard of a talking chicken!"

"Whoever heard of a talking chicken?" Prudence was saying excitedly to her elder sister as they stood by the rabbit hutch. "What shall you teach her next, Abby?"

"Her name, I suppose," said Abigail.

She squatted down again in front of the pullet.

"Pretty Polly," she said. "Come on, Pru, you say it too. Ready? One, two, three . . ." And together the sisters chanted "Pretty Polly" a dozen or so times, till Abigail squeezed Prudence's arm to stop.

They waited.

Then: "Pretty Polly," said the pullet as clear as a bell.

Abigail and Prudence looked at each other with shining eyes. Then Abigail, remembering the scene in the pet shop and forgetting that in fact Polly was only aware of the sound and not the sense of words, said, "What's your name?"

There was no answer.

"Say it again," whispered Prudence, and Abigail said it again and again and again.

When at last she fell silent, Polly put her head on one side, shook it a little as though to clear her thoughts, and then said, "What's your name."

Abigail frowned, thinking.

She only says what I say, she thought. How do I get her to say what I want her to? Her glance fell on the cookie tin in which Benjamin's rabbit mixture was kept. Of course! A reward of food! That was the way. She opened the tin and took out a little handful of the stuff.

Polly watched. "Chuck?" she said hopefully, but Abigail didn't.

"Aren't you going to give it to her, Abby?" said Prudence. "She's been so clever."

"Wait a minute," said Abigail. "Just keep quiet a minute, Pru. Don't say anything."

She sat on the ground, her back against the leg of the old table on which the rabbit hutch stood. Polly waited between her outstretched feet, silent, watching the cupped hand.

"What's your name?" said Abigail.

"What's your name," said Polly.

Abigail shook her head.

"What's your name?" she said again.

"Eat Wheaties," said Polly. "Chuck?"

Patiently Abigail continued to ask the question again and again, but she mostly received the same two replies, sometimes varied with a "Why" and with lots of requests to "chuck," but she never got the answer she wanted.

Still the teacher kept on, and still the pupil kept hoping to be rewarded, till at last Prudence grew tired of keeping quiet and saying nothing and went away.

I won't be beaten, thought Abigail. If only she will say the right thing just once, and then I make enough fuss, I'm sure that will be the break-through.

"What's your name?" she said for the fiftieth time, and Pretty Polly said, "Pretty Polly."

"Clever girl!" cried Abigail.

Quickly she stretched her arm forward, opened her hand, and allowed the pullet to peck hungrily away at the food. With the other hand she stroked the shiny feathers of her striped back.

"Clever girl!" Abigail said. "Clever girl!"

And when the food was finished, she took some more from the tin and prepared to go through the whole lengthy performance again.

But this time, as soon as she asked the question the pullet not only answered correctly but in such a way as to prove to Abigail that here was a chicken beyond her wildest dreams, a chicken to rival any parrot in the land.

"What's your name?" asked the teacher. And the pupil answered, "Pretty Polly. Clever girl!"

CHAPTER 4

"You're a Dutchman"

Not surprisingly, neither the farmer nor his wife believed a word that the children told them about the amazing talking pullet.

"But I heard her," said Prudence.

"And me," said Bob.

"Honestly, Dad," Abigail said. "Polly can talk."

But her father was not the sort of man to put up with such flights of fancy.

"Now, look here, Abby," he said. "We all know chickens make funny noises. But we also know that the only animals that can reproduce human speech are parrots."

"And myna birds," said his wife.

"And budgies," said Prudence.

"And me," said Bob.

"It's all right," the farmer went on, "for Pru and Bob to be making up stories like that, but you're too old to be telling such fibs, Abby. So let's have no more of that silliness. If a hen can talk, I'm a Dutchman."

★   ★   ★

"It's not fair!" said Prudence angrily afterward. "They just didn't believe us. Why don't you fetch Polly, Abby, and make her say something in front of them?"

Abigail didn't answer. She was hurt at being singled out as a liar. But Prudence's question gave her an idea.

She spent the rest of that afternoon with Pretty Polly teaching her something new and rehearsing the pullet until she was word perfect. Then she waited, Polly at her side, until after the milking, when her father had finished washing up in the dairy and came out on his way to the house for tea.

So it was that to his wife's astonishment the farmer came into the kitchen looking very different from his normal cheerful red-faced self. His cheeks were quite pale, and he threw himself down in a chair and passed a hand across his eyes.

"Whatever's the matter, Bill?" his wife said. "You look as though you'd seen a ghost. Here, have a cup of tea."

"I need something stronger, Mary," said Abigail's father in a shaky voice. "She spoke to me."

"Who spoke to you?" said his wife. "Abigail? Prudence?"

"No. It was that pullet. Abby's pet one."

"Polly?"

"Yes."

"*Spoke* to you?"

"Yes. She said 'You're a Dutchman.' "

"You imagined it!"

"Ask Abby. She was there."

Abigail came into the kitchen, Polly at her heels.

"Is this true what Daddy says?" her mother asked. "That bird can actually talk?"

Abigail nodded.

"Listen," she said, and she asked Polly what her name was. Polly answered and was rewarded with a cookie crumb.

The farmer shook his head in wonder.

"I owe you an apology, Abby," he said.

"And me," said Prudence.

"And me," said Bob.

"Yes, all of you. I'm sorry I didn't believe you. Now I'm ready to believe anything."

"Like that Fatso can talk?" said Prudence.

"Oh, no!"

"No, he can't," Abigail said. "Bob thinks he can teach him, but hamsters can't say anything."

"I didn't think hens could."

Fatso was being fed on Bob's lap, and his cheeks bulged with cookie.

"I 'spect he could speak," said Bob, "but he's too polite."

"How d'you mean?"

"Didn't you know?" said Bob. "It's rude to talk with your mouth full."

Just by chance Polly said, "Why."

"What else can she say?" asked the children's father.

"Not much," said Abigail. "Just 'Eat Wheaties.' That was the first thing I taught her. Oh, and 'Clever girl.' "

"She certainly is," said her father.

Polly gave him a searching look.

"You're a Dutchman," she said once again.

"But she only began talking today," said Abigail. "I don't see why she couldn't learn loads and loads of other words."

"She could, couldn't she!" said her father, rubbing his chin in a thoughtful manner. The color had come back into his cheeks, and his voice sounded eager.

He looked at Polly in that critical and observant way that every good stockman looks at one of his animals, assessing its appearance, its condition, its worth.

"She could be a very valuable bird," he said slowly.

"She could be a very unpopular bird," said Abigail's mother, "if she makes a mess on my kitchen floor. Speech-trained she may be, house-trained she is not. Get her out of here, Abby. And you put that hamster back in its cage, Bob, before it's too late."

"It is," said Bob. "He done a poo."

When the children had left the room, their mother looked narrowly at her husband.

"I know you, Bill Brown," she said. "You're as much of a dealer as you are a farmer. Any chance of making a profit out of an animal, you'll sell it. I saw the look in your eye just now, when you said that bird could be valuable. I warn you, don't go getting any ideas about her."

The farmer looked a little sheepish, but he was not cowed.

"Oh, no," he said. "But just think, if the parrot in that pet shop was worth £850, what in the world would that pullet fetch? A talking parrot's one thing, but a talking hen . . . ! Why, that's unheard of, there's never been such a creature, you could ask any price you liked. It's not as though we were all that well off, Mary—it's a struggle on a little farm like this, you know that. The sale of that bird could bring in enough for you to have all kinds of new stuff for the house." And for me to replace the old tractor, he thought.

"No!" his wife said sharply. "Polly belongs to our Abby. She trained her to talk. You're surely not thinking of selling the bird now?"

"Oh, no," said her husband. Not now, he thought. Later, when she's learned a whole lot more words. The more she talks, the more she'll fetch.

CHAPTER 5

A Secret Revealed

Each evening now, as soon as Abigail had done her homework, Polly had to do hers.

So good a natural mimic was the bird that it seemed as though she learned something new every day. At first Abigail taught her simple things, like "Good morning" or "Good afternoon" or "Good-bye." Then she added a number of useful sayings such as "How d'you do" and "Nice to meet you" and "Take care."

Also, because Polly heard the children calling to one another or to their parents, it was no surprise to anyone to hear her shout "Abigail!" or "Pru!" or "Bob!" or "Mum!" or "Dad!"

In addition, because of her great gift for imitation, she soon became expert at mooing like a cow, grunting like a pig, or bleating like a sheep, and could even match the "Cock-a-doodle-doo!" of her father, the big red rooster.

Once Polly had mastered simple remarks, Abigail proceeded to whole sentences and even succeeded in teaching the bird a tongue twister. So that her father was flabbergasted to be told one day by Polly that "Peter Piper picked a peck of pickled peppers."

Nor was he the only member of the family to get a shock. Moss the collie came running to the sound of his name only to find that it was Polly who had summoned him. "Heel!" said the pullet sharply, and he dutifully followed her across the yard, looking dreadfully self-conscious.

There were, however, limits to the pullet's powers.

Though she seemed to retain everything she had been taught, there was no kind of logic to her conversation. In reply to a greeting like "Good morning," she no longer merely repeated those words but was quite likely to say "Clever girl" or "Mum!" or "Moo." And asking her something like "How are you?" might be answered with "Good-bye."

Only one question ever received a correct answer, and that was "What's your name?" Somehow that lesson had stuck, and the reply was always "Pretty Polly." But try as she might, Abigail did not succeed in training her pet in any other form of sensible exchange.

So far, no one outside the family knew of Polly's gift. It had been generally agreed that it must be kept secret.

"Why?" said Bob.

"We don't want strangers to know," said Abigail.

"Why?"

"They might try to steal her."

"Why?"

"Because she's very valuable, Bob," his father said. "The only talking hen in the world, just think of that."

Bob thought about it.

"How many hens are there in the world?" he asked.

"Millions!" they all said. "Millions and millions!"

"P'raps one of them can talk," said Bob.

"Don't be such a silly little boy," said Prudence.

Bob turned very red, a sure sign he was about to lose his temper. When this happened, he always used the same words to show the full extent of his anger, and he used them now.

"BEASTS, DONKEYS, COWS, CATS!" he shouted, and ran from the room.

"That was not very nice, Pru," said her mother. "You're forever calling Bob a silly little boy. That makes you an unkind little girl."

Prudence turned very pale, a sure sign that she was upset.

"You can go and say you're sorry," her mother added, and she followed to make sure that Prudence did.

"There couldn't be another talking hen, though, Dad, could there?" said Abigail.

"No, of course not," said her father, "and that's why you've got to take very special care of that Polly of yours. She shouldn't be running about the farmyard with the other hens—anything could happen to her. She ought to be kept shut up somewhere absolutely safe."

"But Dad, she loves going around with me. She follows me like a dog—you know that."

"Well, that's all right, she can still do that. So long as you're with her, she's safe. I mean when you're at school, for instance, or other times of the day when you might not be around. There's no problem at night—she's shut up with the rest of the flock."

Abigail did not reply because this was in fact not true.

Hatched in the stable, Polly and her brothers and sisters had grown used to sleeping there, and though their mother the old speckled hen eventually returned to the henhouse at night, they did not. Instead, once their wings were fully feathered, they fluttered up to roost on top of the hayracks or mangers or on the high wooden partitions that separated one stall from another.

Abigail knew this; her father did not. So far she hadn't worried about it. Now she did.

I suppose they're not really safe there, she thought. I must shut the stable doors at night. But when she came to do so that evening, she found that she couldn't.

For many years no horse had stood and stamped on the stable's cobbled floor, and the heavy double doors had been left open, sagging with age on their rusted hinges. Now Abigail could not move them.

She thought of catching Pretty Polly to put her somewhere safe, but when she tried to persuade her to come down from her perch, Polly only answered "Abby, Abby, Abby" in a sleepy mutter and would not move.

At that moment Abigail's mother called her to come in. I'll do something about it tomorrow, she thought.

But the next day something happened that put the problem right out of her head. A salesman arrived at the farm, by chance at a time when there was no one around. Farmer Brown had gone to market, Mrs. Brown was out shopping, the girls were at school, and Bob was at his playgroup.

The salesman walked around the yard and buildings calling, "Hello? Anybody around?" But there was no one to answer him. Even Moss had gone with his master.

The salesman, who sold, among other things, chicken food, addressed himself to a large flock of hens that pecked and scratched and clucked around his feet.

"Nobody at home, eh?" he said.

The hens of course took no notice, except for one, a handsome bird with black-and-silver striped plumage, who stood directly in front of him and looked up.

The salesman looked back at her.

"Picked a bad day, didn't I?" he said.

"Peter Piper picked a peck of pickled peppers," said the hen.

CHAPTER 6

The Massacre

Later that day, when the farmer had come back from market, his wife from shopping, and their children from school, the telephone rang. Abigail, who was closest, answered.

Then she called, "Mum!"

"Who is it?"

"Didn't say."

Her mother came to the phone.

"Hello," she said. "My husband? He's milking, can I take a message?"

Later still, when the farmer came in for his tea, she said, "The *Echo* called."

The *Echo* was their local newspaper.

"What about?"

"They want to send a reporter out to interview you. They've heard that there's a talking hen on the farm."

"Who told them? Have you children been telling people?"

"Course not," said Abigail. "I haven't told a soul. I promise."

"And I promise too," said Prudence.

"And me," said Bob.

"No, it was a salesman," their mother said. "One of the reps that sells foodstuffs. Apparently he came out here today when there was no one around, and I suppose Polly must have spoken to him. So he went straight to the *Echo* and told them. And they want to know if there's any truth in it."

"What did you say?" asked her husband.

"I said he must have been drunk."

"And what did they say?"

"They said no, he admitted to having a couple of stiff drinks to get over the shock, but he swore that he had been spoken to by a hen."

"And what did she say?" asked Abigail.

" 'Peter Piper picked a peck of pickled peppers.' "

"Well, that's blown it," said Abigail's father. "I suppose it had to happen sooner or later. That bird's such a chatterbox."

He could not keep a note of satisfaction from his voice.

"I can't wait to see that reporter's face," he said, "when Polly starts chatting to him! You'll be famous, Abby, you will. You'll have your picture in all the papers. They'll want you to go on television, I expect."

"I don't want to be famous," Abigail said. "I wanted it to stay a secret."

"But just think how much she'll be worth once people realize what an amazing bird she is! Thousands of pounds!"

"One, two, three, five, eight, seven, ten thousand pounds!" said Bob.

"But I don't want us to sell Polly," said Abigail in a very quiet, unhappy voice.

Just then the phone rang and the farmer got up to answer it.

"If that's the *Echo,* put them off till the morning, Bill," his wife said. "Say it's not convenient now. We need time to discuss this."

"If you say so, Mary," the farmer replied. He picked up the receiver.

"Yes? Yes, Bill Brown speaking. No, not now, I'm busy. Tomorrow, all right? Okay. See you both then."

"Both?" said his wife.

"The reporter chap's bringing the rep with him. To identify the bird. You talk about discussing this, but the cat's out of the bag, you know. All we can do is wait and see what happens."

★   ★   ★

"Oh, Polly, what will happen?" said Abigail as

35

she said good night to her pet, who was perched on a hayrack in the stable.

Polly looked down at her consideringly.

"How d'you do," she said. And when Abigail did not answer, she said, "Moo! Good morning. Why. Nice to meet you."

Abigail reached up to stroke her.

"I taught you to speak," she said, "and now I can't stop you. If only there were some way I could tell you to keep silent when those people come tomorrow."

"Eat Wheaties," said Polly. "Baaah! Oink! Take care."

Abigail gave the bird a last pat and went out of the stable. She had forgotten having decided she would do something about those open doors.

When she was ready for bed, she stood at her window and looked out across the moonlit yard at the stable, worrying about the day ahead. How could she prevent Polly from talking? She couldn't. Wait, yes she could! She could shut her away somewhere and produce another hen instead. But suppose the salesman remembered her color? Which he would, because she was different from all the other hens in the flock. Except her mother! She was pretty much the same color as her mother. That was it. She would hide Polly and bring out her mother instead, and the silly old thing would just go "Cluck, cluck, cluck."

Abigail got into bed and went happily to sleep.

The fox came at first light.

Abigail was suddenly woken by a terrible din coming from the stable, a medley of frantic cackling and squawking and screeching, and above it all the sound of a well-known voice calling desperately "Abby! Abby! Abby!"

Then there was silence.

Abigail was the first to arrive at the scene, but the others (except for Bob, who slept through all the racket) were not far behind.

And what a scene it was!

Five of the old speckled hen's brood lay dead in a sea of feathers on the cobbled floor—the three red pullets and two of the white cockerels. Of the third white cockerel and of Pretty Polly there was no sign.

"What is it? What's happened?" cried Prudence, clinging to her mother.

"Fox," said her father.

"He's killed them all," said Abigail in a small, flat voice.

You silly girl, her father thought. Fancy letting them roost in here. You've only yourself to blame. The look on her face told him that that was just what she was doing, so he said nothing of it, but went on, "A fox is like that, you see. So long as anything flutters, he'll keep killing—he's programmed to act like that. He would have jumped at them till he panicked them down off their perches right into his jaws. But he may not have got them all, Abby. Look at those feathers."

Abigail looked and saw that all the feathers scattered around the stable floor were either brown or white. Not a single black-and-silver-striped feather was to be seen.

"He couldn't carry more than one bird at a time," the father said, "and we were on the scene too quickly for him to come back for a second helping. My guess is that he's taken the third white cockerel and that somehow Polly's escaped. Maybe she's still in here, perhaps up in the hay-loft."

But search as they might, they found no sign of her in any of the farm buildings. At last every-one gave up except Abigail. Doggedly she hunted on, in the paddock, in the orchard, beyond the little grove, where two white feathers showed which way the fox had gone. She even went right down the farm drive, and it was there at its junc-tion with the main road that she met the reporter from the *Echo* turning in. Beside him sat the sales-man.

"Hello!" said the reporter cheerily. "Hear you've got a talking hen on your farm?"

"A talking hen?" said Abigail. "No, of course we haven't." And that's the truth, she thought miserably. We haven't, not anymore.

"Ah, come on now, young lady," said the salesman. "It was me the bird spoke to. Came out with that old tongue twister about Peter Piper clear as a bell. Dark feathered she was, different from all the others."

At this Abigail remembered her plan to show them Polly's mother.

"We have got one dark bird," she said. "Kind of speckly. P'raps that's the one that's supposed to have spoken to you."

"Show us!" they said.

In the yard Abigail lifted the pophole of the henhouse, and out ran the flock to flap and stretch and scratch about.

"That's her!" said the salesman, pointing to the old speckled hen. "That's the one!" And to the reporter he said, "Got your tape recorder ready? Right, now you just listen."

Solemnly they walked around the farmyard listening, and the tape recorder duly recorded the conversation.

Salesman: "Talk to me, then. Say something."

Speckled hen: "Squawk."

Salesman: "No, speak properly like you did before. Say 'Peter Piper picked a peck of pickled peppers.' "

Speckled hen: "Chook. Squark."

Reporter: "I don't call that talking."

Salesman (angrily): "I tell you she spoke just like a human being."

Speckled hen: "Cluck, cluck, cluck."

Reporter (skeptically): "That's your story."

Abigail (quietly): "Imagine thinking that a hen could talk."

Speckled hen: "Cackle, cackle, cackle!"

★ ★ ★

It was at this precise moment that a movement high in the Dutch barn caught Abigail's eye. Something was squatting between two straw bales, something with black-and-silver-striped plumage and a bright red comb and wattles.

After the mad panic that had sent her scrabbling wildly up to the highest place of safety she could find, Polly was preparing to come down to join the rest of the flock.

The sharp-eyed reporter saw her too.

"Look up there," he said. "There's another dark bird."

"That'll be the one, you'll see!" said the salesman.

The game's up, thought Abigail, but she did not really care, so happy was she to find her beloved pet safe and sound.

"Polly! Polly!" she called, and the only survivor of the speckled hen's brood came fluttering down.

Abigail knelt to stroke her. Not a feather was out of place. Polly had, it seemed, suffered no damage.

"Speak to me, Polly, speak to me!" cried Abigail in her joy and relief, and the salesman nudged

the reporter and grinned in triumph. But no sound
of any kind came from Pretty Polly's beak.

Terror had struck her dumb.

CHAPTER 7

A Handsome Gentleman

Afterward, of course, the rest of the family
wanted to know all about what had happened.

"She'd flown up into the top of the Dutch
barn, had she?" asked Abigail's father.

"Yes."

"And she hasn't been hurt at all?" asked her
mother.

"No."

"What did she say when she came down?"
asked Prudence.

"Nothing. And she hasn't said a word since."

"Why?" said Bob.

"She'd had an awful fright."

"Why?"

"Because the fox came and killed all her brothers and sisters."

Bob's eyes opened wide.

"Killed them all dead?" he said.

"Yes."

"Were they bleedy?"

"Oh, shut up, Bob," said Prudence, "you silly
lit—"

"Pru!" said her mother.

"Tell us about these two chaps, then, Abby," said her father. "The reporter and the rep. What happened when you'd found Polly?"

"They got angry," Abigail said.

"With you?"

"No, with each other. The reporter said to the salesman, 'You've brought me out here on a wild-goose chase, you fool.'"

"We haven't got any wild geese," Bob said.

"And the salesman said, 'You watch your tongue.'"

Bob stuck his out and watched it, staring down past his nose with crossed eyes.

"And then," said Abigail, "the reporter said, 'Talking hen indeed! Why, it's nothing more than a cock-and-bull story.'" And before Bob had time to question this, she went on, "And the salesman said, 'You're asking for a fat lip,'" which made Bob pull in his tongue and stick out his lower lip like a chimpanzee.

"And then what happened?" the others said.

The man from the *Echo* jumped in his car, and off he went with the salesman running down the drive after him shouting, 'Wait for me! Stop! Stop!' But he didn't."

Everybody laughed except Bob, who was still making funny faces, and Abigail.

"Cheer up, Abby," her mother said. "Polly's safe, and what's more, so is her secret."

"But she can't say *any*thing."

"I expect she will—one of these days," Prudence said.

"I'm sure Pru's right," her father said. "Polly's had a nasty shock that's stopped her from talking. Maybe she'd start again if she got a nice surprise."

A surprise was what Abigail got the very next morning.

She had gone to sleep at the end of the day of

the massacre, confident at least that Polly was safe.

In a paved yard in back of the farmhouse there was a big old Victorian dog kennel and run. A high wall bounded one side of the run, and the other three sides were of pointed upright iron bars, too tall and too closely set for any fox to leap over or squeeze through. For perhaps a hundred years no dog had been quartered there, but it had been used on occasion to house various sickly or orphaned animals that needed special attention. Now, at the farmer's suggestion, Pretty Polly was shut there.

And the next morning, a Sunday, when Abigail went to the dog run, she found her pet sitting not inside the kennel but outside in a corner among some weeds that had pushed up through the cracked concrete floor of the run.

Abigail opened the iron gate and went in.

Crossing her fingers, she said, "What's your name?"—the one trigger that had always brought a reply. But none came. Instead Polly stood up, looking rather bemused.

There beneath her, brown and glistening, was her first egg.

Abigail came in to breakfast carrying it very carefully cupped in her hands.

"That's a nice brown egg," said Prudence. "I like the brown ones best."

"And me," said Bob.

"You're not having this one," Abigail said.

"Why not?"

"It's Polly's."

"It's just the same as any other egg, Abby," said her mother. "Put it in the tray in the pantry."

Her father came in, having finished the milking, in time to see Abigail clutching the egg to her chest and saying in a voice of horror, "Oh, no, Mum! We can't eat this one!"

"Why not?" her father said.

"It's Polly's."

"Ah!" said her father. "I though she must be just about to lay. Her comb's a brighter red. But it's just the same as any other egg, Abby."

"But it's Polly's baby!"

Her father smiled.

"Well, not exactly," he said. "But you've given me an idea, Abby. Suppose Polly was able to pass on her talent for mimicry? Suppose one of her chicks inherited it? It's just possible. Now, if I were to buy you a mate for her, a good-looking young cockerel, then a few weeks later we could start collecting a clutch of her eggs. They'd be

fertile by then, and they'd be a better size, too—a pullet's first eggs are always on the small side like this one. I'll see what I can find at market next week if you like."

"Oh. Yes, please Dad. But I still couldn't eat this egg."

"Nor could I," said Prudence.

"I could," said Bob.

Each day that followed, Polly laid an egg in the dog run.

Abigail resigned herself to the fact that they must be used but gave up eating eggs in any shape or form.

"Somehow I just don't like them anymore, Polly," she said. "You understand that, don't you?" But there was no answer. Still Polly made no sound of any kind. Her appetite was good and her behavior normal—she came when called and allowed herself to be petted, and as usual she followed Abigail everywhere around the farm (though nothing would persuade her to go into the stable). But she was mute.

Wednesday was market day, and Abigail arrived home from school agog. Had her father had any luck in finding a suitable mate for Polly? And if so, what would he look like? And what would Polly think of him? And would it be a nice enough surprise to start her talking again?

Soon she knew the answers to all those questions.

"Come and see what I've got for you," her father said. And there outside the dog run was a chicken crate. The farmer opened the lid and took out the occupant.

"What d'you think of that?" he said.

"Oh!" said Abigail. "What a beauty!"

And indeed the new cockerel was a most attractive fellow, his glossy plumage a medley of red and black feathers with touches of bright blue and green. On his head he wore a neat pink comb like a cap, and his curving tail plumes, a mixture of black and olive-green, were long and flowing.

"What sort is he, Dad?" Abigail asked.

"I don't think he's a purebred," her father said, "but I reckon he's got a fair bit of Indian Game blood in him. Look at those long strong legs and his broad chest."

He held the cockerel up, clamping its wings to its sides between his hands, and examined it with a stockman's eye.

"Look at the meat on him," he said, imagining

what a succession of plump Sunday dinners they would breed from this bird.

Abigail looked, but her thoughts were not of broad breasts or juicy drumsticks, but only of Polly's reaction to this handsome gentleman. What will Polly say, she thought, and then, correcting herself, if only she'll say *some*thing . . . *any*thing. She looked at her pet standing silently in the dog run waiting to be taken out for a walk and remembered all the many words that Polly used to say before the fox.

"If only she'd make a noise, Dad. Just to show she still can," she said.

"Let's introduce them, shall we?" said her father. "Open the gate for me."

When the cockerel was put down on the floor of the dog run, he stood for a moment as still as a statue, looking sideways out of one bright eye at Polly, who had retreated to a far corner. Next he shook his head as though to clear it, scratched at the ground, ruffled up his feathers, and settled them again. Then he took several high, mincing paces toward the black-and-silver hen to stand beside her. Like some dandified gallant of old making his bow before a fair lady, he bent his head and, trailing one outstretched wing in the dust, scurried around her with quick small steps. As he did so he gave a string of little hoarse gobbling cries that said as plain as words, "You are without doubt the most beautiful hen in the whole wide world."

Lastly, to complete this courtship dance, he stood on tiptoe, stretched his bright neck to the heavens, and gave a loud ringing crow.

Throughout this display, the watchers noticed, Polly had stood silent, apparently unimpressed, but now, as the echoes of the clarion call died away, they saw her beak slowly open.

Then to their joy Pretty Polly once again found the power of speech, and what is more, it chanced that her choice of words was apt.

"How d'you do," she said.

CHAPTER 8
A Baker's Dozen

There was a good deal of discussion in the Brown family about what to call the new cockerel. Everyone had a different idea.

The farmer said that because the bird looked to have Indian Game blood, it should have an Indian title, so how about Maharajah?

His wife favored Adonis because the cockerel was so beautiful.

Prudence liked Justin because it had very long legs and there was a boy named Justin in her class at school with very long legs.

As for Bob, he had not quite understood that the new arrival was to be a husband for Polly, and thinking it was just another odd-looking hen, suggested naming it Samantha. At which everybody laughed so much that he ran off in a temper, shouting, "BEASTS! DONKEYS! COWS! CATS!"

In the end it was Abigail who chose the name.

"I think he ought to have one to match his new wife's," she said. "She's Pretty Polly, so he ought to be Handsome something—something beginning with *H*."

"Henry?" said Prudence.

"No."

"Hamlet?" said her mother.

"No."

"How about Horatio?" said her father.

"No, no," said Abigail. "He's so noble looking that I think he ought to be named after one of King Arthur's knights of the Round Table. I know, Galahad!"

"But that doesn't begin with *H*!" they all said.

"Doesn't matter," said Abigail. "That's what I want to call him."

So they did.

Handsome Galahad and Pretty Polly now settled down to a life of domestic bliss in the dog run. For various reasons Abigail and her father had decided between them that the honeymooners should not be allowed to range freely about the farm.

First, there was always the possibility of a daytime raid by the fox.

Second, there was Polly's father, the big red rooster, to consider. A meeting with Galahad was bound to result in a fight, and the farmer had no doubt of its probable outcome.

"Just look at those!" he said, pointing to the

sharp curved spurs on the backs of the cockerel's long legs. "He'd knock the old chap out, he would—kill him, probably. And that's no way to treat your father-in-law."

And third, it was important that Polly should grow to regard the dog kennel as her home, where in due course, they hoped, she would hatch and rear her children. To this end, they provided her with a comfortable wooden nest box lined with straw, and though at first she dropped one or two eggs outside in the run or on the floor of the kennel in an absent-minded way, she soon began to lay in the box.

Now that she had Galahad as a protector, the terror of the massacre seemed to have left her at last, and she gradually regained her powers of

speech. At first Galahad was quite obviously amazed to be addressed in a variety of different human voices, let alone hear his wife moo or grunt or baa. But in time he grew used to this phenomenon and would chuckle away in reply as though to say, "Was there ever such a talented hen? Can't understand what she's talking about half the time, but she's brilliant, no doubt about that!"

In addition, he seemed immensely proud of another much more ordinary ability of Polly's: producing eggs. Each morning, when she stepped from the nest box after laying, he would pirouette around her in high excitement and give loud triumphant crows.

Polly also had a way to celebrate this daily event so that no one was left in any doubt that it had happened. Abigail had taught her a new phrase, and anyone who chanced to be near the dog run around midmorning was likely to hear a loud voice shouting, "Three cheers for Polly! Hooray! Hooray! Hooray!"

Many of Polly's early eggs were on the small side, as happens with pullets just beginning to lay, but as time passed they became generally big enough for Abigail's father to tell her one day to stop collecting from the kennel.

"Just leave them in the nest box from now on," he said.

"Why, Dad?"

"So that she can lay a whole clutch, and then with luck she'll go broody and sit on them. A hen's just like any other kind of bird, you see, Abby. Its instinct is to make a nest, lay as many eggs in it as it can comfortably cover, and then sit. Easy for a wild bird, but a domesticated one like a hen finds that every time she lays an egg, someone removes it. So she has to lay another. It's our way of persuading them to produce an awful lot."

"But Dad," said Abigail. "How do we know that Polly will go broody?"

"We don't, and she may well not so early in her first laying season. But she's no ordinary hen, your Polly. And another thing, her old mother's spent half her life stealing away somewhere and going broody. Polly may take after her. We'll just have to wait and see."

So they waited and saw the number of eggs build up until there was a baker's dozen in the nest box. The morning after that they no longer heard the daily shout of "Three cheers!" Looking into the kennel, they saw Polly sitting tight.

Galahad seemed puzzled that his wife would not get out of bed, but every time he approached the nest box inquiringly, Polly fluffed out her feathers and made angry hen noises at him. His feelings were obviously hurt, and he stood there looking injured.

"Thirteen's an unlucky number," said Abigail. "D'you think she'll hatch them all, Dad?"

"She might. There shouldn't be any infertile ones, and she's certainly big enough to cover that many. We shall know the answer three weeks from today."

During those three weeks that Polly was sitting brooding, three things happened among the poultry of the farm. One thing was rather sad, one was downright tragic, and the third, because of the second thing, was a happy chance for the handsome Galahad.

First, Polly's mother, the speckled hen, who was very old, older even than Abigail, fell off her perch one night and died quietly on the henhouse floor.

Next, Polly's father, the big red rooster, was standing one misty morning on his usual crowing place, a fallen apple trunk in the orchard, when the fox sneaked up behind him out of the gloom just as he was preparing to shout "Cock-a-doodle-doo!" and took him by the throat right slap-bang in the middle of the "doodle."

And third, the rooster's death meant that Galahad could now be released from the dog run. He thus exchanged one newly orphaned wife who had taken to sitting doing nothing all day for more than thirty fresh ones, all delighted at the sight of this tall, dark, handsome stranger.

On the twenty-first day Abigail woke very early, wondering for an instant why. Then she looked at the calendar on her wall, showing twenty dates crossed out with a big X, and leaped out of bed.

It really was very early. Nobody was up yet, not even the sun, and the only sounds to be heard were the dawn chorus of the birds and, inside the distant henhouse, the crowing of Galahad.

Abigail opened the iron gate of the dog run and bent down, for the doorway was low, to look into the kennel.

There sat Pretty Polly as usual, hunched over her precious clutch of eggs. She stared at Abigail with a beady eye but made no move or sound.

Curiously, she had uttered no word of the English language during the entire course of the incubation, but only made the sorts of noises that ordinary broody hens make.

Now when Abigail said "Good morning, Polly," she remained silent.

But suddenly in that silence Abigail heard a voice, a very small voice, that was presently joined by other very small voices, until there came from underneath the black-and-silver hen a positive chorus of thin little peep-peep-peeps.

"Oh!" whispered Abigail. "You've done it! You've done it!"

And quietly but clearly the proud mother replied, "Pretty Polly! Clever girl!"

CHAPTER 9

"Three Cheers for Polly!"

Abigail need not have worried that a baker's dozen might prove to be an unlucky number. Later that day, when Polly was persuaded to leave the nest and stretch her legs, there, crouched amid the mess of eggshells that had been their homes, were thirteen baby chicks. Fluffy and bright-eyed, they were all the same size, but it was already plain that later, when they changed their first down for feathers, they would all look very different. Some promised to be the color of their late lamented relations—grandfather, grandmother, or uncles; some of their mother; and some of the father they had yet to see.

The three children stood and looked at the chicks.

"I like the pale ones best," said Prudence.

"And me," said Bob.

"Oh, I don't know," said Abigail. "I think I like the dark ones best."

"And me," said Bob.

"You can't like two things best," they said.

"Why not?" said Bob. "I like them all bester."

"You can't say 'bester.' "

"Why not?"

"Because it's either 'better' or 'best,' " said Prudence.

"There's no such word as 'bester,' " said Abigail.

"There is," said Bob. "You just said it."

"Silly little boy!" cried Prudence.

"Silly big girl!" shouted Bob.

"Stop it, both of you," said Abigail. "You're worrying Polly, making all that noise." And indeed Polly came hurrying back to her babies, and with much clucking and fussing and careful placing of her large feet, settled herself on them. Then she looked up at the children and spoke.

There was seldom any logic to Polly's speech, since she said whatever came into her head, but occasionally by chance she would hit on a happy form of words, and this was such a time.

"Nice to meet you," said Pretty Polly. "Good-bye. Take care."

"D'you think any of the baby chicks will ever talk, Abby?" said Prudence as they shut the iron gate of the dog run.

"Dad said it was possible," Abigail replied. "We'll have to wait and see. After all, they've only just been born."

"I could talk as soon as I was born," Bob said.

"You couldn't!" said Prudence.

"I could so. I said to Mummy 'Hello,' and she said 'Hello, what's your name?' And I said 'Bob, and I'm hungry and what's for tea?' "

Abigail laughed.

"Well, I know what's for tea today, Bob," she said. "Something you like."

"Cookies?" said Bob.

"No."

"Cupcakes?"

"No. Crumpets."

"Yummy," said Prudence. "I love crumpets."

"And me," said Bob. "They're bester than anything." And he ran off to the house as fast as his short legs would carry him.

In the days and weeks that followed there was no obvious sign that Bob's legs had grown any longer, but the change in Polly's chicks was very noticeable. From pretty little balls of fluff they had become lanky and gawky, and their soft down had been replaced by stubby feathering. They ran around in great excitement whenever Abigail came to the dog run and greeted her with a variety of sounds. As had happened with Polly, "peep" gave way to "cheep" and then to "chick," but more than that they never said, despite Abigail's efforts to teach them. In fact, they had two teachers, for Polly also seemed to be eager that they should learn to talk. To be sure, she spoke mainly to them in hen language, but Abigail often heard her telling them what Peter Piper picked or calling for three cheers or asking them how they did. But no word of the Queen's English issued from any of those thirteen beaks.

As time passed it was plain that the dog run was just not big enough for fourteen birds, and at night the kennel was jam-packed.

"We're going to have to let them out with the rest, Abby," her father said. "You'll have to train Polly to go to roost in the henhouse at night. She'll follow you there if you call her, and the youngsters will follow her."

"But what about daytime, Dad?" Abigail said. "The fox might come again."

"They'll just have to take their chance like the rest of the flock. After all, they're only thirteen ordinary young cockerels and pullets, no different from any others, because it doesn't look as though any of them are going to talk."

"Polly didn't talk till she was four months old," said Abigail. "And anyway, Dad, even if we let them out, couldn't she stay in here? She's absolutely safe here."

"But would she be happy?" her father said. "That's what you have to ask yourself. It's a bit like a prison cell in here, isn't it? Not as bad for her as life is for a wretched commercial farm hen, but think how much happier she'll be outside, running about freely again with her mate and her chicks and all the other hens on grass instead of concrete, with loads of insects and worms to peck at. Okay, there's a risk, but I think we should take it."

"But Dad," said Abigail, "you keep saying that Polly is very valuable."

"She is," said her father. "She's unique, a total freak, there's never been another hen like her. She's the Eighth Wonder of the World. And I confess I began by just thinking how much money we could get for her. But I don't feel like that anymore. She's your pet and I know how fond of her you are, and that's more important to me than any amount of money. All the same, I think she should have her freedom."

"What do you think, Polly?" said Abigail. "Shall I let you out?"

"Eat Wheaties," said Polly. "Good afternoon. Moo! Baa! Oink! Oink!"

"That's not much of an answer," said Abigail. "Looks as if I'll have to make my own mind up." And she opened the gate of the dog run.

"Clever girl," said Pretty Polly.

She marched out of the run with all her thirteen children, and they followed the farmer and his daughter across the paved yard and around the side of the farmhouse.

Now they could all see, beyond the buildings, the green grass of the orchard. Here Galahad and all his other wives were pecking and scratching happily about in the sunshine, and at this sight Polly grew very excited.

"Three cheers for Polly! Hooray! Hooray! Hooray!" she shouted, and she followed this up with a loud recitation of all the words that Abigail had ever taught her, ending with the name of her husband.

"Galahad! Galahad!" yelled Polly at the top of her voice, and at this, Abigail and her father could see, the distant cockerel looked up from his foraging, gave a loud ringing crow, and came running at top speed on his long legs.

"What a performance!" said the farmer. "I never knew you'd taught her so much, Abby. Good thing there's no one around, or that would surely have given the game away."

What he had not noticed was that under cover of the racket that Polly had been making a car had come up the drive.

"Galahad!" shouted Polly once again as her husband came racing across the barnyard. And then, once more getting her words right by sheer luck, "How d'you do, Dad?"

"Did you hear that!" said the farmer.

Suddenly behind him there was the thunk of a car door closing.

"Did you hear *that*?" said Abigail.

CHAPTER 10

The Duke

They looked around to see that a Land Rover had drawn up outside the stable. From it a tall thin man came walking toward them. He was quite elderly, they could see, with a long face like a horse and a long nose, and he wore a tweed jacket of an old-fashioned cut, and knickers above long woolen stockings and brown leather boots. On his head was a shapeless tweed hat, which he swept off as he reached them.

"Do forgive me," he said to Abigail's father, at the same time making a little bow in her direction, "but I wonder if you could do me a favor."

"I daresay," said the farmer. "What's the trouble?"

"Nearly out of diesel," said the tall old man. "Not enough to get me home, and I can't find a garage anywhere that keeps the stuff. Wonder if you could be kind enough to sell me a drop?"

"Certainly," said the farmer. "Glad to help. My name's Brown, by the way. Bill Brown."

"Charlie Severn," said the other.

All the time that they were talking there was a

babble of noise from Polly at being reunited with her husband, and from her thirteen children and their father at this first meeting. But Abigail waited anxiously for her father to take the stranger off to where the fuel was stored. At any moment, she feared, Polly might come out with one of her remarks in front of him. Indeed, she was standing in front of him now, looking up at this oddly dressed figure with her head on one side. Abigail held her breath.

"By Jove, that's a handsome bird," said the tall old man.

"That one's my daughter Abigail's pet," said the farmer.

"Abigail, eh? Charming name. One of my favorites."

Taking off his hat again, the tall man held out his hand.

"How d'you do, Abigail," he said.

"How d'you do, Mr. Severn."

"Well, I'm not a mister, in fact, doncherknow. I mean, don't let it worry you, Abigail, but actually I'm the Duke of Severn."

"Oh," said Abigail.

"So now each of us knows what the other is called," said the Duke, "except for this handsome hen. What's your name?"

And at this familiar question Polly answered loudly and clearly, "Pretty Polly."

For a moment there was such a silence that if it hadn't been for the gabbling of Galahad and his children and the bawling of calves and the bleating of sheep and the barking of Moss, you could have heard a pin drop.

Then, "By Jove, that was cleverly done!" said the Duke of Severn. "Mind if we try it again? This time I'll watch you really closely." And when Abigail did not answer because she did not understand, he said once more, "What's your name?"

And once more the hen replied, "Pretty Polly."

"Remarkable!" said the Duke. "Never saw your lips move at all. Always been fascinated by ventriloquism since I was a boy. Always longed to be a ventriloquist myself. But I was never much good, doncherknow. And 'Pretty Polly' is jolly difficult to say, I should think. And the way you threw your voice—why, it really seemed as though that hen was actually speaking! Remarkable!"

"Clever girl!" said Polly.

The Duke of Severn stared at Abigail with an expression of pure delight on his long-nosed face.

"I should jolly well think you are clever, Abigail," he said. "Never known any of the professionals to do it as well—you can always see their lips move a tiny bit if you watch carefully. You've got a prodigy here, Mr. Brown, d'ye know that?"

"Er, yes," said Abigail's father. He had never actually met a duke before and wasn't sure how to address one. He had an idea he should have said "Yes, Your Grace," but that seemed a funny thing to say to an old chap who wanted to buy a couple of gallons of diesel, so he didn't.

"Ought to be on television," the Duke went on. "She'd make a fortune with that hen. Brilliant idea, that—a ventriloquist performing with a live animal as a dummy. Knock all the other fellows for a loop."

All the time that the Duke was talking, Abigail and her father were thinking the same thing. He might be fooled now, but unless they could get rid of him quickly, sooner or later Polly would wander off and say something at a distance, too far away for Abigail to have possibly thrown her voice.

They both spoke at once.

"I'll take Polly on down to the orchard," said Abigail, and "I'll go and fetch that diesel," said her father, and walked hurriedly away.

"Come, Polly," said Abigail.

It'll be quicker if I carry her, she thought, the others will follow. She held out her arms and the bird fluttered up into them.

As Abigail turned and hastened away, Galahad and his thirteen children following, Polly's head poked up over her shoulder.

"Peter Piper picked a peck of pickled peppers," she called.

The Duke of Severn stood alone, lost in thought and admiration.

Remarkable, he said to himself. Could almost have sworn that as the child spoke the bird moved its beak in time with the words.

At that moment Bob appeared in the barnyard carrying Fatso the hamster, and seeing a stranger standing there, marched up to him and said with his usual directness, "Who are you?"

The Duke took off his shapeless hat once more and, bending down, gravely shook hands.

"Charlie Severn," he said. "You'll be a brother of Abigail's, I daresay? What are you called?"

"Bob," said Bob, "and this is Fatso. I wouldn't shake his hand. He'll bite you."

"Is he yours?"

"No, he's Abby's, but I look after him and my sister Pru looks after Benjamin the rabbit 'cause Abby's busy with Polly, you see."

"Yes, I've just been meeting Polly," the Duke said. "Your sister Abigail is very clever, you know. Anyone would swear that that hen of hers was really talking."

"Well, it is," said Bob. "Didn't you hear it?"

"Of course, of course!" said the Duke, smiling.

Just then Abigail returned from the orchard.

"Tell him, Abby," said Bob. "He doesn't believe that Polly can talk," And he trudged off wearing a look of scorn that anyone could be so foolish.

"What fun!" said the Duke. "Your little brother is really taken in. He genuinely believes the bird can speak."

"Yes," said Abigail. Then quickly, as she saw her father approaching, she said, "Here's Dad with the diesel."

When the Land Rover had been filled up and the fuel paid for and the Duke of Severn had once more doffed his hat and shaken the hands of father and daughter, he climbed into the driver's seat and folded his long stockinged legs under the steering wheel.

"Very many thanks," he said to the farmer. "You've been most kind."

"Glad to be of help, Mr. . . . I mean, er, Your . . . that is, sir," said Abigail's father.

"And as for that act of yours, Abigail," the Duke said, "I've never seen such a piece of voice-throwing! 'Peter Piper picked a peck of pickled peppers,' eh! And to use a live hen as a dummy, clever idea, I mean if the fox gets that one, why, you've got plenty more, one hen's just the same as another, right? Well, must be getting along now. Any time you and your father are anywhere near Severnside Castle, do come and see me. You might feel like giving me a lesson."

"Thank you," said Abigail.

The Duke started his engine. Then he said, "I say, just before I go, would you do something for me, Abigail? Would you just say the old ventriloquist's test piece, the one they always reckon is the hardest? I've never been able to do it. Will you say it?"

"Say what?" said Abigail.

" 'Bottle of beer.' "

Abigail kept her lips absolutely still and, trying not to allow her throat to be seen to move at all, said, "Gottle of geer."

The Duke of Severn's long horse face broke into a smile.

"You're pulling my leg, right?" he said. "You're just pretending that you can't say it. You can't fool me." And with a final wave he drove away.

CHAPTER 11
Galahad to the Rescue

Abigail had no trouble training Polly and her family to roost with the rest of the flock at night. That same evening she went out just before dusk and called Polly to the henhouse.

"And they all went in like lambs," she said afterward.

"Lambs couldn't get through that pophole," said Bob. "They're too big."

"It's just an expression, Bob," his mother said. "It means they went in quietly."

"Lambs aren't quiet," said Bob. "They're always making a row, silly things, wanting their mummies."

"Like you," said Prudence.

Bob began to turn red in the face, but before he could utter his usual cusswords, his father said, "Don't be so catty, Pru," which made Prudence turn pale and Bob return to his normal color.

"Meeow," he said under his breath.

"Just stop it, you two children," said their mother. And to Abigail she said, "I expect Galahad's glad to have Polly back, isn't he?"

"Oh, yes," Abigail said. "They perched side by side just like a pair of lovebirds."

And indeed in the days that followed it was plain that while Galahad might now have a great many wives, Polly was his favorite by far. Every night they sat together on the perch murmuring sweet nothings to each other until they fell asleep; in the daytime, as the flock ranged about the barnyard and the orchard, Galahad was seldom far from Polly's side.

One fine day a month or so after the Duke of Severn's visit it happened once again that none of the family was at home. Abigail and Prudence were at school, the farmer and Moss had gone to market, and Mrs. Brown was shopping while Bob was at playgroup. But this time it was not a man selling foodstuffs who came up the farm drive but a dog looking for something to eat.

A lean wolfish mongrel it was, a stray with no collar and no owner and no food in its belly and no hesitation about chasing the first chicken it saw in the barnyard. By chance this was one of Polly's children, and though it ran for the orchard as fast as it could, the dog was faster, and it began to look as though thirteen would be an unlucky number after all.

By another chance Polly was not around but

was sitting in a nest box inside the henhouse about to lay an egg. And the rest of the flock of course simply exploded left, right, and center in a perfect panic of squawks and screeches and frantic flappings.

All except one.

The dog had caught up with the fleeing bird and was gripping it by one wing when its wretched victim's cries for help were suddenly and dramatically answered.

Galahad came racing across the orchard on his long powerful legs, his ruff raised, his wings spread, seeming in his fury to be twice his normal size. He was traveling at top speed when he hit the dog, and despite the difference in weight, he bowled it over. It gave a yell of surprise, while its quarry, released, ran thankfully away.

The dog was not done, though. It picked itself up and seeing, as it thought, just another chicken in front of it, leaped growling at Galahad.

Polly, her egg laid, came out of the henhouse at this point to see her husband apparently about to meet his end at almost exactly the same spot (had she known it) where her father had met his. What chance had Galahad against an animal twice the size of a fox?

The answer was soon plain.

Galahad's Indian Game blood was boiling, and
as the dog rushed in, Galahad jumped above it and
slashed at its back with his cruel razor-sharp spurs.

Once, twice more, the dog ran at the cockerel,
and each time the jaws snapped and missed, and
the spurs struck and ripped.

Suddenly the raider had had enough. Tail
tucked tightly between its legs and yapping with
terror now, it fled, bleeding from a dozen
scratches, while Galahad sped it on its way with
a final flurry of pecks.

Proudly the victor returned, flew up onto the orchard gate, flapped his wings, and crowed his triumph to the world and his wife. She in her turn saluted her hero, with words which, perhaps fortunately, he could not understand.

"Galahad!" she cried. "Clever girl, Galahad!"

Nothing of this drama was known to the Browns, although Abigail did find a scatter of feathers beside the old fallen apple trunk in the orchard and also noticed that one of the baker's dozen looked rather disheveled. It was a young cockerel, and though Abigail hadn't given much thought to the sexes of Polly and Galahad's offspring, her father had.

"You realize," he said at breakfast one day, "that out of the thirteen birds that were hatched in the dog kennel only three are pullets. The other ten are cockerels, and you needn't think we're going to keep all that lot, Abby. There are ten Sunday lunches there. We could have one this weekend."

"Oh, Dad!" cried Abigail. "I couldn't eat one of Polly's children!"

"I could," said Prudence.

"And me," said Bob.

"I like roast chicken," said Prudence.

"And me," said Bob.

When Abigail was upset, she neither colored like her brother nor paled like her sister. Her distress signal was a trembling of her lower lip, and this her mother now saw and quickly said, "Why not sell the cockerels, Bill? That's the best way out of it."

Her husband was about to dispute this, but then he too saw that Abigail was far from happy.

"All right," he said. "I'll take 'em to market next week."

Abigail looked happier at this, Prudence and Bob less so.

"What are we going to have for Sunday lunch, then?" asked Prudence.

"Oh, a nice piece of beef," her mother said. "Or perhaps a leg of lamb. Or roast pork."

"Good," said Bob. "I like all of them bester."

At market a salesman who saw that Farmer Brown had a pen of cockerels for sale came up and introduced himself.

"I sell all types of poultry food," he said. "Perhaps I could have the pleasure of your business. I'm new to the area, you see."

"Thought you were," said the farmer. "I used to deal with a different chap in your firm. What's happened to him?"

"He . . . er . . . took early retirement," said the salesman.

"Oh?"

"Yes, had a kind of a nervous breakdown."

"Overwork?"

"Not exactly. He had an experience that preyed on his mind. Kind of hallucination, I suppose. He couldn't forget it, and of course it affected his work. Happened on a farm around here somewhere, not sure which one."

"What was this experience, then?" asked the farmer.

The salesman laughed.

"Shame to poke fun at the poor chap, really," he said, "but he went around telling everybody that he'd been spoken to by a hen!"

CHAPTER 12

Grace

Abigail sat on the trunk of the old dead apple tree, thinking. In front of her Pretty Polly and her three remaining children scratched and pecked for a handful of corn that Abigail had thrown into the long grass. Polly was in her farmyard-noise-imitation mood, bleating or grunting or mooing as she found each grain, but the three pullets just clucked.

Six months old now, thought Abigail, and not one of the baker's dozen has ever uttered a word. Perhaps it was because there were so many of them that I couldn't teach them anything. But now there are only three, so maybe I'll be able to get through to them. And they're females, too.

Abigail did not actually believe that girls were more intelligent than boys. Quieter perhaps, and more helpful in the classroom, and not always fighting or showing off. But there was no doubt that in general female creatures were cleverer than males when you thought about it. They could do so many things that males couldn't, like having

babies and having milk to feed them with and, in the case of birds, being able to lay eggs.

"You jolly well ought to be able to talk," she said to the three pullets. "Oughtn't they, Polly?"

"Eat Wheaties," said Polly.

"Clever girl!" said Abigail. "Of course! That's what I started you on, wasn't it! I should have remembered." And she spent the next hour doling out more corn a few grains at a time and repeating "Eat Wheaties" again and again.

But the pullets only clucked.

Each of the three sisters was different. One was white, one was red, and one was exactly the color of the grandmother she had never known—her gray feathers covered in a host of rusty-brown spots.

There was something in the look of this last bird that made Abigail feel she was probably the most intelligent of the three. She seemed to be paying attention to Abigail's instructions about eating Wheaties while the other two did not, and occasionally she made a noise that was different from theirs. It was still a chicken noise but a distinctive one. It sounded like "chook."

Abigail came to a decision. The smaller the class, the better results a teacher should expect to get, and surely there was nothing to beat a one-on-one relationship. From now on she would concentrate all her efforts on the speckled pullet.

Like their mother, the three pullets were very tame and would come running when Polly's name was called and allow themselves to be petted or picked up in a way the rest of the flock would not tolerate. But if the speckled pullet was to be privately tutored, she must have a name of her own and be trained to answer to it. What should it be?

Abigail was considering the matter when she heard her mother calling, "Abby! Where are you?"

"Here!" Abigail shouted.

Her mother appeared at the orchard gate.

"Quick," she called. "You're wanted on the telephone."

Abigail ran toward her feeling distinctly alarmed. Who could it possibly be? She hated answering the phone anyway, and if it rang when her parents were not handy, she would leave it to Prudence (who was bossy and nosy and liked to speak) or even Bob (who loved to pick up the receiver and always said the same thing very loudly in case the person was a long way away, which was "THIS IS BOB BROWN AND WHAT DO YOU WANT, ANYWAY?").

"Who is it?" she said as she reached her mother.

"I don't know. A man with a rather elegant voice asked for Miss Abigail Brown."

Inside the house Abigail took up the receiver gingerly, as though it were a poisonous snake.

"Hello?" she said nervously.

"Miss Abigail Brown?" said the elegant voice.

"Yes."

"Ah, good morning, miss. This is Severnside Castle speaking."

For a moment the form of words meant nothing to Abigail, and then she thought, It doesn't sound much like him, but it must be the Duke calling. What do I call him?

All she could think of to say was, "Oh, hello. How are you?" So she did.

"In excellent health, I thank you, miss," said the voice, sounding now both elegant and amused. "This is the Duke of Severn's butler speaking."

"Oh," said Abigail.

"His Grace would like a word with you, miss. Would you be good enough to hold the line one moment?"

"Oh," said Abigail. "Yes."

There was a pause, and then a familiar clipped voice said, "Hello. Abigail?"

"Yes."

"Charlie Severn here. How are you?"

"Fine, thanks."

"Good. Splendid. And how's Polly?"

"She's fine."

"Still 'talking,' is she, ha, ha?"

"Yes."

"Remarkable, that act of yours. Haven't been able to get it out of my head. Which is why I'm calling, Abigail. I have a favor to ask of you. I mean, you'll have to consult your parents about this, of course, but I've been wondering . . . think I told you when we met how keen I've always been on ventriloquism . . . never was any good at it, but of course never been properly taught, doncherknow. I wonder, would you consider giving me lessons? I would pay for your time and trouble, of course."

"Oh," said Abigail. Oh, help, she thought, what can I say? I can't give him lessons in something that I can't do.

"Tell you what," said the Duke. "Suppose I just pop over in the old Land Rover—I'll make sure she's got a full tank this time!—and we can have a chat about it. Saturday morning suit you? Won't be at school then, will you?"

"No."

"So that will be all right, will it?"

"Yes."

"Splendid!" said the Duke. "By Jove, I can't wait to start learning the tricks of the trade."

"What shall I do?" said Abigail later, when she had reported the conversation to the family.

"He's coming this Saturday, did you say?" her mother asked.

"Yes."

"You'll just have to make a clean breast of it,"

her father said. "No good going on pretending. Anyway it wouldn't be fair—to anyone—doesn't matter if it's a duke or a garbageman."

"What's a duke?" Bob said.

"A nobleman."

"Are you a noble man, Daddy?"

The farmer laughed.

"No," he said, "I'm a commoner."

"Commoner than who?" Bob said.

"Daddy means he's just an ordinary person," said Mrs. Brown.

"He's not!" said Bob. "He's bester."

"He means he's like everybody else. Dukes aren't ordinary."

"Well, how d'you get to be a duke?" asked Prudence.

"You have to be the eldest son of the previous duke," said her father. "And then when your father dies, you become the next duke. If I was the first Duke of Brown, then when I died, Bob would become the second Duke of Brown."

Bob looked pleased at this idea.

"That's not fair," said Prudence. "He's younger than me."

"Oh, for goodness' sake!" said Abigail. "I still don't know what I'm going to say to him on Saturday."

"Always tell the truth," her mother said. "You can't do better."

"You'll feel better about it, too," her father said. "After all, we did rather play a trick on the old chap, didn't we?"

For the three days that remained before Saturday, Abigail worried.

She worried about having tricked the Duke, because she rather liked him.

She worried that once he knew Polly's secret everyone would know.

And she worried because she didn't know what to call him.

This third worry served to put an end to a fourth one, however—what to call Polly's speckled pullet.

"That butler called him His Grace," she said to her. "What am I going to call you?"

"Chook," said the speckled pullet.

"I know!" said Abigail. "You shall be my Grace!"

She was in fact in the middle of giving Grace a lesson in the stable when on Saturday morning the Land Rover drew up outside. Abigail had chosen the stable as a classroom for Grace's private instruction simply because Polly still would not set foot inside it. Which was convenient, because it meant that lessons could go on without continual interruptions.

Abigail picked Grace up and came to the stable doorway to see the Duke of Severn getting out. He was wearing exactly the same strange old-fashioned clothes as before, except that instead of his squashy tweed hat he had on a brown bowler.

"Abigail!" he cried, sweeping it off and giving a little bow. "Good morning! Who's that you've got there? Looks a bit like Polly, but not quite the same color. What's this one's name?"

"Grace," said Abigail. "I mean . . . um . . . this is my Grace, Your Grace."

The Duke's long face broke into its slow smile.

"I think I see what you mean," he said. "But look, don't call me Your Grace."

"Well, what should I call you?" said Abigail.

"Call me Charlie. That's my name."

"I don't think I could," said Abigail.

"Oh, well, just call me Duke," said the Duke. "Is that all right?"

"Yes. Duke."

"So you're Grace," said the Duke of Severn, stroking the pullet's speckled back.

"Any relation to Polly?"

"Yes," said Abigail. "She's Polly's daughter."

"You needn't have told me yourself, Abigail," said the Duke. "You could have thrown your voice and made Grace tell me."

"I couldn't," said Abigail.

"Why not?"

Abigail gulped, and then all in a rush she said, "Because I can't throw my voice, Duke . . . I'm not a ventriloquist at all, you see, you just thought I was when you saw me with Polly, and I let you go on thinking that because I didn't want you to know Polly's secret."

"Which is?"

"She can talk. She can really talk."

"That's what your little brother Bob said."

"Yes. She talks just like a parrot, you see, only more than any parrot, I expect, because I've taught her so many things. But it's not me that's clever, it's Polly, and that's why I can't give you lessons, Duke, and that's the truth."

"Always tell the truth," the Duke said. "You can't do better."

"That's what Mum said."

"Your mother is right," said the Duke. "And I understand everything you're telling me, though I can't quite take it in, doncherknow. A hen—

talking like a parrot! Quite remarkable! Any chance you could get Grace's mother to demonstrate this gift of hers for me?"

"I expect so," said Abigail. "She's probably out in the orchard. I'll just have a look."

Still carrying Grace, she went back into the stable again. In its rear wall there was a small window, a barred window without glass in it, which looked directly out into the orchard, and after peering through it, Abigail called to the Duke. "Yes, she's out there. With Galahad."

"Who's Galahad?"

"Her husband."

"Grace's father?"

"Yes. Come and listen. She's sure to say something soon." So they stood at the window and looked out and listened.

It was a fine still morning, the kind where sound carries from a long way away, and they could clearly hear all the noises of the farm, and in particular the comfortable chuckling and clucking of the flock as they foraged in the orchard grass. Then Galahad leaped on the apple trunk.

"Listen," whispered Abigail. "That's his special crowing place, and Polly always says something when he crows, though it won't make sense."

And sure enough, Galahad flapped his wings and stretched his neck and, looking proudly around his domain, cried his loud challenging call.

As the echoes died away, "Abigail! How d'you do. Nice to meet you! Take care! Good night!" shouted Pretty Polly.

"Remarkable!" said the Duke of Severn. "Never have believed it! And she can say other things, too, Abigail?"

"Yes, Duke. Loads of things."

"And what about your Grace here? You training her, too?"

"Yes. But I'm not having any luck."

"Doesn't she say anything?"

"No. She does make one noise that's a bit different from her two sisters, but it's not a real word. I'll see if I can get her to say it now."

She put Grace down on the stable floor and said, "Come on, Grace. Say something for our visitor."

The speckled pullet looked up at the tall thin figure in his tweed jacket and knickers with a bright considering eye.

Then loudly and clearly she said, "Chook!"

"Not a real word, you say?" said the Duke of Severn. "Why, she actually said my title!"

CHAPTER 13
Inside the Henhouse

At this, Grace made her special sound once again, and this time it seemed to Abigail that it did sound more like "Duke!" than "Chook!"

"That's the noise I was meaning," she said. "She's been saying that for quite a while."

"She must have been calling for me," said the Duke of Severn. "She was telling you that she wanted to see me."

"Oh, I don't know," said Abigail doubtfully.

"I'm joking," said the Duke. "At least I think I am. But I must say she seems to have taken a bit of a fancy to me." And indeed the speckled pullet appeared to have quite forgotten Abigail and was staring up at the tall old man with a look of great interest, while now it was hardly possible to doubt that what she was saying to him was indeed "Duke! Duke! Duke!"

To cap it all, she fluttered up into his arms.

"I say, Abigail," said the Duke as he stroked the bird, "I suppose you wouldn't . . . no, no, of course you wouldn't."

"Wouldn't what?"

"Well, I mean, I realize that you wouldn't sell Polly."

"Oh, no! Never!"

"But would you consider selling Grace?"

"To you, you mean?"

"Yes. She seems to like me, and I certainly like her, she's beautiful, never seen one quite that color before, remarkable. And by Jove, you know, if she can say one word, that may not be much compared with her mother, but it's one word more than any other hen in the world. And there's always the chance she could learn one or two more. And it suddenly occurs to me that I could use her as I thought you were using Polly when first we met—as a live dummy! I could have the greatest fun, you see—once I'd practiced enough—taking her around to local shows and fetes and charity do's—I can just see it: 'Special attraction. His Grace the Duke of Severn and his Grace. Step right up! Step right up!' Why, you never know, we might end up on television! What do you say? Will you sell her to me?"

Abigail said nothing, because she did not know what to say.

Grace said "Duke," because that was all she could say.

The Duke said "Pity," because he had had a moment's vision of himself as the successful ventriloquist he had always wanted to be. But he could now see that Abigail was not at all happy with the notion of parting with Grace, so he hastened to reassure her.

"It was just an idea, Abigail," he said. "Forget it. I can see you don't want to sell her." And he handed the pullet back.

Just then they heard another car pull up, and Abigail went to the stable doorway to look out.

It was the reporter from the *Echo*!

Seeing her, he came over and said, "Hello, young lady, got another 'talking' hen?"

Abigail said nothing.

The Duke said nothing.

Grace said nothing.

"I was just passing," said the reporter, "so I thought I'd drop in. Funny thing, you know— that salesman chap that came out here with me before, he was just imagining things, of course, off his rocker. But he must have told a good number of people, because I keep coming across stories of a hen that can talk. No smoke without fire, eh?"

Oh, thought Abigail, oh, Duke, please don't

say anything, please don't tell him about Polly. It'll be in all the papers and we shall never have a moment's peace.

The reporter from the *Echo* addressed the Duke.

"Have you heard these stories, may I ask?" he said.

Abigail held her breath and Grace's beak.

"I certainly have not," said the Duke of Severn.

"You'll be this young lady's granddad, I dare-say?"

"I certainly am."

"And you can assure me that there is no talking hen on this farm?"

"There certainly is not."

"You sure?"

"Young man," said the Duke. "Are you call-ing me a liar?"

"No," said the reporter hastily. "No, sir. Of course not."

"I suggest you take your leave."

"Pardon?"

"Push off! Get lost! Beat it!" said the Duke of Severn.

Abigail looked at him as the sound of the re-porter's car died away.

"Always tell the truth," she said. "You can't do better."

The Duke grinned.

"I'm a very wicked old man," he said.

You're a very kind old man, thought Abigail, telling whoppers to keep my secret.

She held Grace out to him.

"Please, Duke," she said. "Take her. She's yours."

"Do you mean you didn't ask him any money for the bird?" her father said afterward.

"Not everyone's as mercenary as you, Bill," his wife said.

"I'd have asked him for lots of money," said Prudence. "Dukes are rich, they must be, the Queen is married to one. I'd have asked him for loads."

"And me," said Bob. "I'd have asked him for a hundred and twenty-ten pounds."

"But you just gave her to him?" asked her father.

"Well, sort of," said Abigail. "More lent her, really. I said I'd take her back if she wasn't any good."

"Any good to eat?" said Bob.

"No, no," said Abigail, and she explained why the Duke wanted Grace.

"And he said we must all come and spend a day at Severnside Castle before too long," she said.

"Is it a real castle?" asked Prudence.

"Yes, he was telling me it's got turrets and a drawbridge and a moat and a herd of deer in the park. Oh, and a butler."

"What's a butler?" asked Prudence.

"Someone who buttles," said her mother, laughing.

"Like that old ram we had once with the curly

horns?" asked Bob. "He buttled me in the bottom once."

And at that they all laughed so much that Bob, who didn't see what was funny, ran away shouting, "BEASTS! DONKEYS! COWS! CATS!"

That night, when Abigail went to shut the flock up, she opened the side door of the henhouse and went inside.

Polly and Galahad were sitting together in their usual place, and Abigail made her way to them through the perched rows of warm, sleepy murmuring fowls. She began to stroke Galahad down his long silky ruff and over his broad back and along the length of his sweeping tail feathers, and he made soft gurgling noises of pleasure. To Polly she said, "What d'you think? Grace has gone to live in a castle."

Without fail the act of speaking to Polly would prompt a reply in human, not hen, language, sometimes a senseless one like "Heel!" and sometimes an apt one like "Good night, Abigail." But now Polly only fluffed out her feathers and chirred at her owner in a grumpy way.

Funny, thought Abigail as she latched the henhouse door. Anybody would think she was angry with me for letting Grace go.

In bed Abigail worried about this. It was so unlike Polly to behave this way. Suppose she had suddenly lost her gift of speech? After all, it had happened before, after the massacre in the stable.

The following night Abigail went once again to the henhouse, anxious to have Polly reply to her, to show they were still on speaking terms.

It was a little later than her visit of the previous evening, and she had brought a flashlight. Shining it now through the gloom, she picked out the figure of Galahad, his head drawn down into his shoulders, his long tail hanging below the perch. But he was sitting alone. Has Polly fallen out with him, too, thought Abigail, and she shone the flashlight along the perches in turn, and on the floor, and into each of the nest boxes.

But Polly was not there.

CHAPTER 14
The Fete

They searched the farm buildings, but there was
no sign of her.

In the morning they searched the yards and the
orchard and the paddocks and even the far fields,
but Polly was nowhere to be found.

Abigail was heartbroken.

"Oh, Dad," she said at last, "she must have
been taken, mustn't she?"

She could not bring herself to add "by the
fox," but her father knew what she meant and
thought it very likely that Polly had ended up as
a square meal for one of the red raiders. Though
in fact, he thought, we've not found any evidence
of that. No sign of a struggle, no scatter of black-
and-silver feathers, no blood.

"It looks bad, Abby," he said. "But she had
some happy times, didn't she? Better than being
shut in that old dog run, eh?" And when Abigail
did not answer, he gave her a big hug, and then
she had a good cry.

"There'll never be another hen like Polly!" she

sobbed, and to this there was no answer, for it was patently true.

"Pity Abby let that speckled pullet go to the Duke," he said to his wife later. "She might have trained her to say something."

"It isn't just the talking," his wife said. "She really loved Polly. It wouldn't have mattered if she'd never said another word. It's hit her hard, poor girl."

Prudence and Bob were of course aware of Abigail's unhappiness at the loss of her pet.

"I expect you'd like to have Benjamin back now, wouldn't you, Abby?" said Prudence.

"No," said Abigail listlessly. "You can have him."

"For my own?"

"Yes."

"What about Fatso?" asked Bob.

"You can have him, Bob," said Abigail, and when the new hamster owner had gone off bursting with pride, she said to Prudence, "You can help him with feeding and cleaning up, can't you?"

"Oh, yes," said Prudence. "And thanks, Abby. But couldn't you get Polly's daughter back?"

"From the Duke, you mean?"

"Yes."

"No. It wouldn't be the same. Anyway, I told him he could keep her if he wanted to."

And indeed it was soon plain that he did want to.

A couple of days later a letter arrived, the envelope addressed MR. AND MRS. WILLIAM BROWN, MISS BROWN, MISS PRUDENCE BROWN, AND MASTER ROBERT BROWN.

"Who in the world's this from?" mused the farmer.

Prudence looked over his shoulder.

"They haven't put Abby's name in," she said.

"Let's see," said her mother. "Ah, yes, that's the old-fashioned way, you see. It's because Abby's the elder girl."

She turned the envelope over. Its flap was stuck down with sealing wax, the wax impressed with a crest of arms.

"It must be from your noble friend, Abby," she said. "You'd better open it."

Inside there was a copy of a typewritten flier which said that on a Saturday in two weeks' time the villagers of Dumpton-on-Severn would be holding their annual fete on the grounds of Severnside Castle by kind permission of the Duke of Severn. There would be games and pony rides and all kinds of sideshows, including a juggler, a fortuneteller, and a ventriloquist. At the bottom of the notice was a penned message. It said:

DO COME. GRACE AND I MAKE A GREAT TEAM. C. S.

"I don't think I want to go," said Abigail.

"I do!" said Prudence.

"And me!" said Bob.

"Oh, come on, Abby," her father said. "It'll make a nice day out."

"It'll take your mind off things," her mother said.

For Prudence and Bob the two weeks before the fete flashed by.

For Abigail the days dragged.

Everybody seems to have forgotten about you now, Polly, she said miserably to herself. I'd have expected Galahad to be missing you like mad, yet he doesn't seem to be. But I do.

When the day of the fete came and they all arrived at Severnside Castle, the first person they saw was a majestic figure of a man. Large and portly and red-faced with carefully plastered down hair and wearing a wing collar, a black

jacket, and pinstriped trousers, he sat at a little table beside the main gates, taking entry fees.

"I thank you, sir," he said as Farmer Brown handed over the money. "Enjoy your day." There was no mistaking that elegant voice.

"Was that the Duke?" Prudence whispered.

In fact, the Duke was nowhere to be seen. They went to all the sideshows, and Prudence and Bob had pony rides.

"Don't you want a ride, Abby?" her father said.

"Not really," said Abigail.

"Well, come with me to the fortuneteller then," said her mother.

"Oh, all right."

The fortuneteller sat in a little dark tent with a crystal ball on the table in front of her. She stared into it for some time without even looking at Abigail, and then she suddenly said, "You've lost something."

"Yes," Abigail said. Then she made herself ask, "Will I find it again?"

The fortuneteller did not answer. Instead she stared into Abigail's eyes for what seemed ages, and then slowly and dramatically she said, "Sometimes it rains cats and dogs. But not always."

"Whatever did she mean, Mum?" Abigail said afterward.

"Goodness knows," her mother said. "I don't expect she's a real fortuneteller. Probably the butler's wife."

"But she knew I'd lost something."

"That's a pretty safe thing to say. Everyone loses something now and again."

Last of all the Brown family came to the ventriloquist's tent. It was quite a big one, and outside it there was a notice. It said:

THE FAMOUS VENTRILOQUIST SIR LAUGHALOT
AND HIS AMAZING TALKING HEN!
PERFORMANCES EVERY HALF HOUR

Abigail's father looked at his watch.

"It's getting on half past three," he said, so they waited outside the tent, and soon a little line formed behind them.

"Where's this Duke?" said Prudence as they stood there. "I haven't seen him yet."

"You soon will," said her father.

Once inside they sat facing a little curtained-off stage. Then the curtains were drawn back to reveal a strange and unexpected scene.

Sitting on a chair in the middle of the stage was a figure dressed from head to toe in a suit of armor. The armor had apparently been designed for a much shorter man, for it fit very poorly, with great gaps here and there, but the helmet the figure wore was a particularly fine one, topped by a white horsehair plume. The visor was down so that the face could not be seen. On one mailed fist stood Grace.

"Good afternoon, ladies and gentlemen," said the ventriloquist in a voice that Abigail instantly recognized, even though it rang hollow within the

helmet. "May I introduce Grace, the amazing talking hen! Say hello, Grace."

There was a pause, and then in high-pitched

tones equally hollow the Duke's voice said, "Hello."

It was obvious to anyone where the second voice was coming from, even though the Duke jerked his fist a little as Grace "spoke," so that she had to give a kind of bow to keep her balance.

"Now, then, Grace," said the Duke in his ordinary voice, "why did the chicken cross the road?" Then in the high voice he replied, "To get to the other side, of course," while jiggling Grace up and down in time with the words.

And in this manner the show went on, laced with a whole series of dreadful jokes.

Some knew and some suspected that it was the Duke of Severn himself inside the suit of armor, but no one laughed, because the jokes were so feeble.

As a display of ventriloquism, it was embarrassingly, pathetically bad. Only a small child could possibly have believed that the replies came from the mouth of the speckled hen. (Indeed, on the way home Bob announced that he had liked the man in the armor "bester than anything else.")

The Browns, having been first in, were the last to go after the act ended, and before they had left the tent the armored figure came clanking down from the stage and took off its helmet.

"Phew!" said the Duke of Severn, producing a handkerchief from within his breastplate and mopping his brow. "It's jolly hot in here!" And he bowed in his courteous way and gave a mailed handshake to Mrs. Brown and Prudence, whom he had not met before.

"What did you think of it?" he said to Farmer Brown.

"Oh . . . er . . . very good," said Abigail's father. "Grace behaved very well, didn't she?"

"Didn't she just! Just let out one shout of 'Duke!' halfway through, but then she nearly always does, haven't got her to say anything else yet. Good dodge of mine, wearing that armor, don't you think, Abigail? Got several suits of the stuff in the banqueting hall, doncherknow. Suddenly thought, by Jove, with a helmet like that on, no one could possibly see my lips move! Smart idea?"

"Yes," said Abigail.

"Well," said the Duke, "it's very good of you all to come and support our fete, and I hope that soon you'll come and spend a day here by yourselves and I'll show you around. Now if you'll excuse me, I must get ready for my next performance."

He bowed and turned away, but as they were leaving the tent, Abigail heard him call her name. She went back in.

"When you do come, Abigail," said the Duke, "bring Polly. I'd love to see her again."

The words brought such a lump to Abigail's throat that she could only nod. So would I, she thought. So would I.

CHAPTER 15

A Sudden Shower

Some days after the fete at Severnside Castle, Abigail looked at the calendar on her bedroom wall and realized that it was now a whole three weeks since Polly had disappeared.

When, she wondered, would she ever get over the pain of missing that familiar voice? Galahad might crow his head off and the rest of the flock greet her with their customary cluckings and cacklings, but those were all just chicken noises. What would she give to hear once again those distinctive tones. And to think how many words Polly had been able to say—the only hen in the world to speak the Queen's English, the only hen, it now seemed, who ever would, for Grace really only said "chook," whatever the Duke might think.

She got out of bed and went to the window.

It looked as though it was going to be a horrible day, the sky filled with angry clouds that threatened heavy showers. Altogether it would be a silly idea to go out early that morning before sunrise, but for some reason that she didn't quite know, Abigail decided to get dressed and go outside.

She was not, of course, the first up. Already she could hear the hum of the milking machine, and downstairs her mother was moving about in the kitchen. But Prudence and Bob were still fast asleep, as she saw when she peered into their bedrooms. They both looked very happy.

Prudence lay on her back, a little smile at the corners of her mouth.

Bob lay curled up on his side facing the hamster cage, which stood on his bedside table. He had more of a grin on his face, Abigail thought, he'd probably gone to sleep with it there after a last look at his pet. If she could see inside the nest ball, Fatso was probably grinning too. I wish I could be happy again, she said to herself as she pulled on her boots.

She was halfway across the barnyard when the shower started, and a heavy one it was, too. The rain came bucketing down, and she ran for the shelter of the Dutch barn. Sitting there in the dry on the bed of straw at the bottom of the great sloping cliff of bales stacked up behind her, she stared out at the rain until the shower had passed. Suddenly, now that the noise of the downpour was over, she thought she heard a hen cackle.

I must have imagined it, she thought, for the flock had not been let out of the henhouse, but then it came again. It seemed to be somewhere above her.

Abigail got to her feet to look up, and as she did so there was a movement at the mouth of a kind of little dark cave between two bales, about halfway up the stack, and all of a sudden something came falling down.

It fell quite slowly, as though it was very light, landed on the soft straw bed with a little bounce, and got to its feet, quite unharmed.

As Abigail looked up again another little something came tumbling down, and then there was a positive shower of them falling around Abigail.

"Sometimes it rains cats and dogs. But not always," the fortuneteller had said, and she was right! It was raining chicks!

And finally a familiar figure appeared at the mouth of the little cave and came fluttering down the cliff of bales and landed among her babies and called them to her.

"Cluck, cluck, cluck," said Polly to her children, Polly who, when last seen, had fluffed out her feathers and chirred angrily at Abigail because

she was extremely broody and ready, the very next day, to begin to sit on the clutch of eggs that she had laid secretly high in the Dutch barn. Each day of the three weeks that had passed since then she must have slipped down for a little while to feed and drink and then fluttered back up again, seen by no one. And now they were hatched, and every one had made a happy landing.

Abigail was speechless. Big tears of joy ran down her face, and she stretched out a hand to stroke the black-and-silver striped feathers.

But Polly had never been lost for words, and this time they could not have been better chosen.

"Hello, Abigail!" said Pretty Polly. "Good morning!" And at that a great golden sun came swimming up over the distant hills and shone on them, warm and welcoming.

It was going to be a lovely day after all.

DICK KING-SMITH was born and raised in Gloucestershire, England. He served in the Grenadier Guards during World War II, then returned home to Gloucestershire, to realize his lifelong ambition of farming. After twenty years as a farmer, he turned to teaching and then to writing the children's books that have earned him many fans on both sides of the Atlantic. Inspiration for his writing comes from his farm and his animals.

Among his well-loved novels are *Babe: The Gallant Pig, Harry's Mad, Martin's Mice* (each an American Library Association Notable Book); *Ace: The Very Important Pig* (a *School Library Journal* Best Book of the Year); *The Toby Man,* and *Paddy's Pot of Gold.* Additional honors and awards he has received are a *Boston Globe–Horn Book* Award (for *Babe: The Gallant Pig*) and the California Young Reader Medal (for *Harry's Mad*). In 1992, he was named Children's Author of the Year at the British Book Awards.